101 STORIES OF 2+1

MADHURI JOSHI

INDIA • SINGAPORE • MALAYSIA

ISBN 979-8-89133-904-0

Dedicated to

ANIKA, our love!

Preface

We are a happy two. The plus one in our lives has brought in so much more joy! She is our little rockstar.
We cherish these four years of 2+1! Dad, Mom and Anika's joyride filled with cheer, wit and love.
This 2+1 have many fun stories to share! So here we go...

1

Hello World!

Anika in the tummy- knock, knock.... I can't wait to meet you all!
Mom and dad- please wait for some more time baby!!
Anika (pops out)- hello world!!

0.1

2

Kangaroo family!

In NICU, to keep our tiny human warm..
Kangaroo mother care, KMC
Kangaroo father care, KFC
They called us a Kangaroo family!

0.1

3

She is like a!

The other end of phone- how is the newborn baby sir?

Dad- she is like a tender cucumber!

Mom- she is like a *chot menshinkai*!

Dad- she is like a baby rat!

Mom- she is like a freaking frog!

0.1

4

Little Durga

NICU: Her first vaccination. And not a single grimace on her face. That moment I knew this newborn is a fighter! For all the strength our preterm has shown, I call her our little DURGA Devi!

0.1

5

Cow, calf and bull

The first few months, the only job I was doing and was expected to do was to feed Anika. I couldn't stop from identifying myself with a cow and baby with a calf. Eating greens and milking colostrum. And of course loving the bull.

0.2

6

Special *tottillu*!

Baby Anika using the same *totillu* that baby mom had used 30 years ago. Slightly renovated.
Some things are indeed special!

0.2

7

Malish and massage

Anika baby getting nice *malish* and massage everyday by the maid.
It's as good as a spa!
Mom to dad- Why am I not a baby?!

0.2

8

Baby *Bharatanatyam*

Anika baby's favorite past time was to move her upper limbs vigorously in a highly co-ordinated manner. It was like watching a *bharatanatyam* show! Baby *bharatnatyam*!

0.2

9

Emojis

Anika would give 101 expressions as a baby.
Mom would capture them and use them as Emojis!

0.3

10

Picture of calm!

During all the functions,
Other babies- cry, throw tantrums and create a storm
Anika- smiles and is a picture of calm

0.4

11

What's in a name?!

Anika is a combination of Anila and Kala, her grandparents.
It is the name of Goddess Durga.
It means brilliance in Sanskrit, gracefulness in Latin, unique in Arabic, beauty from inside out in Australian.
All that her Mom and Dad want her to be and more!

0.4-forever

12

Baby Gym!

Anika had a baby gym where she would “exercise” vigorously. To pep it up, mom would play music and match it with baby’s moves. And live telecast it to dad. Our rockstar didn’t disappoint at all!

0.4

13

A hundred reactions!

We started Anika's supplementary feeds with fruit pastes.
Mom made boomerang videos for each fruit...
A hundred tastes, a hundred reactions!

0.5

14

Anikaversary

First anniversary after Anika was born.
Everyone wishing mom and dad- "Happy ANIKAVERSARY"

0.6

15

Half birthday!

Half year around the sun.
Half way to one.
Half birthday cake done!

0.6

16

Pierced!

Baby Anika got her ear pierced.
Ear piercing ceremony for the baby is the next painful thing for a mother after delivery.
It's like piercing mom's heart directly!

0.6

17

Those laughters!

Dad and daughter have these laughter sessions together.
And each time mom sees them laugh....
Mom *Heart melts*

0.6-infinity and beyond

18

Sensitivity testing

Mom gives little amount of food to Anika like a test dose prior to an antibiotic.
Anika doesn't like it.
Dad marks it as an 'allergen' in the sensitivity testing!

0.7

19

Sucking

Anika sucking her fingers.
Mom- what's so delicious baby, stop sucking your fingers!
Anika *Does a full asana and starts sucking her toes*

0.8

20

Photoshoots

Baby in sunflower field…
Baby 'hanging out'…
Baby getting makeup done…
Baby on the clouds…
Baby at the beachside…
Baby pizzeria…
Mom did all sorts of photoshoots for our little supermodel!

0.1-0.11

21

Waiting for my turn!

Anika(8m)- appa

Dad *yeah!!!*

Anika(10m)- appa appa

Dad *coudnt stop smiling*

Anika(12m)- appa appa appa

Dad *exploding with happiness*

Meanwhile, Mom in the background *waiting for her turn impatiently!!*

1.0

22

Monthly birthday!

Every month I would decorate the number of month with flowers and take pictures.
Baby Anika would know “Mom got flowers, I think its my monthly birthday today!”

0.1-1.0

23

Kisses!

One on the forehead, one each on the cheeks, one on the nose and one on the chin.
Ask Anika for 1, and you get 5 kisses!

1.0-I hope forever

24

Little steps!

The first time she took those little steps, it left footprints in our hearts.
One step at a time, I hope she conquers the world!

1.2

25

What doctor?

Someone- "Anika, dad is what doctor?"
Anika- *Touches her head*
Luckily, they didn't ask her what doctor mom is!!

1.2

26

Fill in the blanks!

Little Anika would sing rhymes in her toddler voice.
She would sing a few sentences and for those she didn't
know, she would go…tra lalala
We had to fill in the blanks!

1.5

27

Abababaaba

Anika had picked up saying *'abababa'*.

It would be funny when it was used at the right time.

For example:

"Dad loves mom"

Abababaaba.

1.5

28

Generational change

Mom and dad started using youtube at 18 years.
Anika started using youtube at 18 months.
Talk about generational change!

1.6

29

Baybee

What does dad call mom??

Anika- Baybee

With a grin on her face!

30

Toddler playlist

Mom would always listen to some romantic playlist on a drive with dad.
Baby enters the scene- Dad play rhymes!
So on a drive, the playlist goes like this…
' the wheels on the bus….
Johny johny yes pappa…
Are you sleeping…
Pavadisu paramatma…'
Mom in the backseat-ZZZZZZ

1.6-??

31

Swing and slide

Her perfect playdate was/is...
Swinging and sliding...in the park.
Mom and dad being her spectators!
She can spend the whole day playing!

1.6

32

Voice modulation

Dad- Anika

Anika- Dad

Dad- Anikaaaa

Anika- Daaaad

Dad- ANIKA

Anika- DAD

Perfect voice modulation!

What Talent at that age!

1.7

33

Surprise!

There was a video in which they show an Egg and say ‘open, open…surprise’

One day later…

Mom asking Anika alphabetical words.

Mom- E for….

Anika- Open open…surprise!

We were definitely surprised by the answer!

1.8

34

What is your name?

Dad (holding a capsicum in hand)- which vegetable is this Anika?

Anika

(looking at it for a whole long minute, confused, asks the capsicum)- what is your name?

1.8

35

Modern guru

We asked Anika to identify colors.
She goes- Red... pink....yellow....white...blue...black... violet...
Both of us looking at each other- "violet??? Who even taught her"
Then we see Youtube, the modern guru on screen!

1.8

36

Mini car

Anika has a mini car which functions just like a car!
Every six months, it undergoes servicing- tyre change, engine tuning, gear repair!
Bill as BIG as a big car!

1.9

37

Anita ‘o’ Anita

Anika hadn’t learnt saying ‘KA’ yet.
And there was this song ‘Anita o Anita’ on her “toddler playlist” in the car.
So when she was asked what her name was…
She would say Anita.
Mom would not leave the scene without correcting it to Anika, Afterall it’s such a wonderful name!

1.11

39

Favorite toys

Talking tom and dancing cactus.
Whatever she says is repeated. So fascinating for the little one.
Hands down her favourite toys among hundreds of toys.

1.11

40

Why?!

Why do toddlers do this to parents??!!
At home- smile and laugh
Outside- howl and cry

2.0

41

Rhymes on mind

Mom and Dad discussing… "Let's go to HAMPI"
Anika- are we going to HUMPTY dumpty sat on the wall??
Rhymes on her mind, all the time!

2.0

42

Brush your teeth

Brush brush, brush your teeth.

Other children- *keep their head still and move their brush*

Anika- *keeps the brush still and moves her head vigorously*

2.1

43

Huh?

Anika- ncjheiuwhubndj
Dad- What did you say?!
Anika- ncjheiuwhubndj
Mom- huh?
Anika- *Throws a tantrum*
Just because we didn't understand!

2.2

44

Alexa doesn't understand!

Dad- Alexa play 'wheels on the bus'

Alexa plays wheels on the bus.

Anika (in her baby voice)- alexa play 'wheels on the bus'

Alexa doesn't play.

Anika repeats again. Alexa doesn't play.

Anika- this alexa doesn't understand! ANIKA play 'wheels on the bus'

plays it herself

2.4

45

Made my day

Anika would go to play home and her ma'am would send videos of her.
Mom would enjoy seeing those videos in free time at work place.
It would make my day!

2.4

46

Big girl now

Mom- Anika you are a small girl. You should not be doing it. Anika standing next to the height chart- “Look, look I am such a BIG girl now”

2.5

47

Role play

What Anika enjoys the most??
Role play!
"Dad you are mom
Mom you are Anika
And I am dad."
Ok now, lets talk!!

48

Techniques of feeding

Different techniques of feeding the toddler at different times:

6-12 months- Showing dogs, cats and cows

12-18 months- Watching videos on youtube

18-24 months- Telling ghost stories

24-30 months- Giving her special offers!

0.6-2.6

49

Little singer

Anika has turned out to be a wonderful little singer.
And Mom just loves it!
It is one of those “What parents couldn’t, they want their kid to do”

2.6

50

Aksharabhyasa

The first things Anika wrote on a silver bordered slate was:

A aa E ee

A B C D

1 2 3 4

I hope with the help of these letters she frames beautiful words that conquers hearts!

2.6

51

School interview

Online school interview:
Anika was asked to name the things shown on the screen.
First picture popped up…
An all excited Anika- PIG PIG PIG
…many questions followed, excitement continued and she was selected!
Pig saved our day!!

2.6

52

I will eat for you

Mom trying to convince Anika to eat a fruit
"You will eat or I will eat for you"

2.7

53

Complaint box

"Mommy didn't buy me ice cream"
"Mommy didn't take me to the play area"
"Mommy didn't listen to me"
Anika had this complaint box that she would open up the moment dad came home!

2.8

54

Aquatic creature

Anika playing in water 24/7
With all the mess around, Mom to herself- She must have been an aquatic creature in her last *janam*!

2.9

55

Baby love

Anika has a soft corner for babies.
Being a tiny tot herself, it is so heartwarming to see her pamper little babies.
All heart!

2.9

56

White like paper

Dad- Why are you writing on sofa?

Anika- Because its white like paper.

Mom *Imagining buying a new sofa already!!*

2.11

57

Toys everywhere

Anika picks up toys wherever we go.
Not even a single toy set is in perfect shape, size and/or number.
Such is the state of affairs!

2.11

58

Water baby

Other kids:

After bath, come out of the bathroom

Anika:

After bath, sits in the tub for an hour!

I told you, she is a water baby!

2.11

59

Animal love

"Mom I want to cuddle that dog"
"Mom that calf is so cute"
"Dad look at those colorful fish"
"Dad I want a pet at home"
Our little sweetie loves animals!

2.11

60

Same school

Anika attending the same school in the same campus which dad had attended. Decades later.
Nostalgic indeed!

3.0

61

Strength and weakness

Anika's weakness- the three Cs- Choclate, ice Cream, Cake. So these are automatically mom's strengths.
If mom wants anything to get done, the three Cs are the offers!

3.0

62

School hazard

Till she was 3- not even a common cold!

At 3- *joins school*

'Cough, cold and fever' every alternate week!!

School hazard till the tiny tots develop herd immunity.

3.0

63

Torch to sun

Dad takes Anika to paediatrician
Anika to paediatrician- doctor uncle, Carrot is good for the eyes, please eat them!
Medical advice to doctor himself!
It's like showing torch to Sun!

3.1

64

Write A

Mom and dad in childhood:

"Write A"

Mom and dad- *wrote A*

Cut to now,

Anika- One slanting line, one more slanting line, one sleeping line.

3.2

65

Jana gana mana

Dad buys a tricolour cupcake for Anika on independence day.
Anika- This cupcake is “jana gana mana” in color

3.2

66

Baby 1 & 2

Anika looking at my boobs and pointing out
Baby 1 and Baby 2
"When will the babies burst and come out mommy"

3.2

67

It's not working

Mom- Play with the kitchen set

Anika- its not working mommy

Mom- Anika give me the remote

Anika- its not working mommy

Mom- Wash your hands in the sink

Anika- its not working mommy

The newly learnt "Its not working" had become an excuse!

3.2

68

Cool it down!

Anika had her bumb against the fridge door.
Apparently it will cool it down!!
How I wish it could work for adults too!

3.3

69

Drawings

Anika loves drawing and coloring.
She draws cartoons, nature, hearts and some super sweet family pictures like the cover of this book.

3.3

70

Good ghost, bad ghost

Apparently ghosts are good or bad depending on their color.
White ghost is a good ghost
Black ghost is bad
Yellow ghost is a friend
Red ghost is love ghost
Which color ghost do you like?

3.4

71

I am not here

Dad- Do homework Anika…

Anika- I am not here dad.

3.4

72

Parent's condition

Mom and dad trying to show her talent.

"Anika sing *Ramaskandam...*"

Anika- Its not night yet to sing *Ramaskandam*!

Parent's condition every time.

3.4

73

TV kalyanam

Mom, Dad and Anika watching Srinivasa *kalyanam* on TV.
Anika- *puts *mantrakshati* to TV*
TV *kalyanam*!

3.5

74

Red hot chilly

Fancy dress competition, had to dress her up as something red.
First thing that comes to my mind for this naughty girl is...
Chilly, RED HOT CHILLY.
So all dressed up, she goes on stage and tells..
“I am a red hot chilly
I am too spicy
If you eat me, you should drink lots of water
Hotty hotty, spicy spicy”

3.5

75

Can't fool them

Mom trying to convince Anika to eat fruits.

Mom- see baby K told she likes to eat banana.

Anika- what?! Baby K can't talk no!

You can't fool these kids!!

3.5

76

Happy birthday hanuman

Hanuman *jayanti,*

Anika has an anglisized wish for Hanuman.

'Happy birthday to you Hanuman, may God bless you'

Mom- Hanuman is only God right, then why may God bless you?

Anika- Because Lord Ram is Hanuma's God!

Mom- *stunned by the answer*

3.6

77

Gentle reminder

Some say Anika resembles my mother-in-law.

Whenever Anika is not in a good mood and hits mommy, its like a gentle reminder from the heavens!

My mother-in-law reminding me to take care of Dad well!

3.6

78

Touching the not

Anika-Which plant is this?
Mom-Touch me not
Anika- I am touching the not mommy!

3.6

79

Govinda!

Japas, *Mantras* and *bhajans*.

The little *bhakt* of ours was so into it that the only thing we could hear in the house at one point of time was-

"Srinivasa venkatesha"

"Narayana narayana"

"Sri Ram jai Ram, jai jai Ram"

Govinda Govinda!

3.6

80

Shantha Clause

It's Christmas time!
Anika- will Shantha clause come mommy?
Mom- Yes! we need Shantha clause (peace clause) at home baby!
Peace!

3.6

81

Pooja room drama!

Mom doesn't give her what she wants.

Anika goes straight to pooja room. With folded hands, in a dramatic way,

"*Srinivasa, venkatesha*! Look what my mom is doing to me. She is not giving me ice cream. Please give her some *buddhi*. I'll come to meet you again in Tirupathi"

3.7

82

They are friends!

Mom- Wear your undie and then pant Anika

1 hour later, goes to pee.

Anika- Mom, look both undie and pant are friends, they are coming out together!!

3.7

83

Blanket game

Anika- *hides under the blanket*. Asks me to tell dad to search her.
Dad- where has Anika gone, lets search....and here she is!
Anika- *laughs her heart out*
It amazes me how these little games entertain the toddlers every single time!

3.8

84

Eggs and sperms

Anika- how was I born?

Dad trying hard to explain eggs and sperms to a toddler!

Mom (looking at her lovingly)- I cannot imagine any other egg and sperm to have made our darling baby.

3.8

85

Pre-school effect

Sharper, stronger, meaner
And more social…
Once Anika started going to pre-school.

3.8

86

Potty lessons

Mom gets confused between potty and pee!

Anika- look mommy, pee means susu or no.1

Potty means yaya or no.2.

Got it??

Early morning free vocabulary lessons for mom!!

3.8

87

Your baby, my baby

Just to tease my little one, me holding my niece,
"She is my baby"
Anika - Mom let's do one thing- baby K is my baby and I am your baby. Okay??!!

3.9

88

Her bffs!

Pinky, Bluey, Pubbly are her bffs.
They have hot water bath every day.
They eat what we eat every day.
They sleep in their warm nursery every day.
They play with Anika every day.
And one of them have their birthdays every day!!!

3.9

89

Assigning genders

Anika assigning genders to morning activities!

Anika- I want to pee. She's urgent.

I want to poop. He's coming.

3.9

90

She got me!

Mom- baby listen to me, I'll tell you one thing, please can you do it for me?
Anika- ok tell me where should I pose for the photo.
She got me!

3.9

91

What's going on!

Apparently when Anika is behaving well, she resembles dad.
And when she is behaving not so well, she resembles mom.
Like what's going on!!

3.9

92

Warning

Mom doesn't listen to Anika.

Anika throws a tantrum.

After one hour-

Mom suggests something that Anika doesn't like.

Anika gives a WARNING- "Look mommy, I'll throw a tantrum again!!!"

3.11

93

Those questions

Anika's questions that I probably expected MUCH later:
Why have you and dad made me?
What is the difference between girls and boys?

.

.

.

What is life??!

3.11

94

First gist

Mom- Let's see who takes bath first today. Dad or you?

Anika- Mom, please no first gist.

Got it my girl!

3.11

95

Expressive

Anika has turned out to be such an expressive little girl. She narrates incidents so animatedly and with so much emotion, that the scene just comes alive!
Our little heroine!

3.11

96

Typical pre-term

Milestones- Fast
Hyperactive and smart
Lean and mean
Wants things done as soon as she asks
She is a typical preterm!

0.1-4y

97

Pretty pretty

It's so cute to match those lovely baby dresses with those pretty clips, bows and headbands.
Final product- A very pretty looking girl and a beaming mom!

0.1-always

98

Dad or mom?

Anyway we asked the most frequently asked question to kids:
YOU LIKE DAD OR MOM?

Year 1- Dad

Year 2-Dad only, I don't like Mom

Year 3- When Mom is there, I like Mom. When Dad comes back, its Dad

Year 4- Dad and Mom both.

Mom- Finally!!!

1.0-4.0

99

Caress

A habit Anika had as a baby and has it to this day?
This weird sweet habit of caressing our hands
while drinking milk.

0.1-now

100

Total timepass

She laughs
She frowns
She jumps
She plays
She loves
She fights
She is our total timepass!

4.0

101

You are the best!

Anika- mom you have 2 mouth, 3 eyes, 4 ears

Mom- You mean I am special baby?

Anika- yes mom, you are the best!!

Hugs and kisses followed!

4.0

Other books by the author:

About the Author

Dr. Madhuri Joshi was born to doctor parents in Ballari. Obstetrician, Gynaecologist and infertility specialist by profession, she is married to her college batchmate, Dr. Arun MA who is a Neurosurgeon. They are blessed with a daughter, Anika. Settled in Bengaluru, her other interests include cooking, travelling, music, photography.

Previous Books by Madhuri Joshi

FUN

Intended

MADHURI JOSHI

... A tribute to a woman I Love

MADHURI JOSHI

www.ingramcontent.com/pod-product-compliance
Lightning Source LLC
LaVergne TN
LVHW041118150826
845673LV00007B/2114